For the girls, Jillian, Olivia, Brodie and Gwennie—MW
To Arthur and Hugo—high fliers!—AJ

LITTLE HARE

www.littleharebooks.com

Little Hare Books
an imprint of
Hardie Grant Egmont
Ground Floor, Building 1, 658 Church St
Richmond, Victoria 3121, Australia

www.littleharebooks.com

First published 2007
First published in paperback 2008
Reprinted 2009 (twice)
Reprinted 2010
This edition published 2013

Cataloguing-in-Publication details are available from the
National Library of Australia

ISBN 978-1-742975-52-8

Designed by Kerry Klinner, Megacity Design
Cover design by Hannah Robinson, Xou Creative
Additional design by Hannah Robinson, Xou Creative
Produced by Pica Digital, Singapore
Printed through Asia Pacific Offset
Printed in Shen Zhen, Guangdong Province, China

5 4 3 2 1

LUCY GOOSEY

MARGARET WILD & ANN JAMES

Ever since she was a fluffy gosling with flippy flappy feet, Lucy Goosey had lived in this pond.

She had jumped off that branch
sticking out of the water.

She had sat on that rock as big as a cow.

And she had played hide-and-seek in those bushes,
dark as caves.

Now Lucy Goosey was nearly full grown. She had proper feathers, and she had even learned to whiffle her wings as she landed in the pond.

'What good whiffling, Lucy Goosey!' said her mother.
'You will find it very useful during our long flight.'

'I don't want to go,' said Lucy Goosey.

The time had come for all the geese—Lucy Goosey,
her mother, her cousins, her aunties and uncles—
to fly away to another country. They were leaving
that very night, as soon as the sun went down.

Lucy Goosey stared up at the sky.
It was vast. Never-ending.

'I'm not going!' she said, and off she ran on her flippy flappy feet.

'Come back, Lucy Goosey,' called her mother, 'or you'll get left behind.'

'Don't care,' honked Lucy Goosey.

'Don't care,

don't care,

don't care!'

Lucy Goosey crept into the bushes, dark as caves.
She hid among twigs and leaves.

She tucked her head under her wing, so she couldn't
hear or see a thing.

She must have fallen asleep, because when she squeezed out of the bushes, it was night time. And very quiet.

Lucy Goosey hurried down to the pond.
It was empty. All the geese—even her mother!
—had gone.

Lucy Goosey swam around in lonely little circles.

Then she huddled in the reeds,
listening to leaves rustling,
twigs cracking, things slithering.

'Mum?' she whispered.

Suddenly there was the sound of wings whiffling and a long, sad honking—'Lucy! Lucy Goosey, my dear, where are you?'

'Mum!' said Lucy Goosey, and she sped out
of the reeds faster than a flying fish.

Her mother held Lucy Goosey close. She said, 'What's the matter, Lucy Goosey? Why don't you want to leave?'

Lucy Goosey stared up at the sky.
It was dark and mysterious and never-ending.

'What if I lose my way in the
misty moisty clouds?' she asked.

'If that happens,' said her mother, 'I will search the misty moisty clouds until I find you.'

'What if I am caught in a storm
and get tossed into the tree tops?'
asked Lucy Goosey.

'If that happens, I will search every
tree top until I find you.'

'What if I get tired and fall into the cold, dark sea?' asked Lucy Goosey.

'If that happens, I will search the cold,
dark sea until I find you.'

'Will you always search for me?' asked Lucy Goosey.

'Always,' said her mother.

'Even when you're *old?*'

'Even when I'm old.'

'When you're very old,' said Lucy Goosey,
'*you* might lose your way and be scared.'

'I might,' said her mother.

'If that happens,' said Lucy Goosey,
'I will look everywhere—
in the sky, on the land,
in the sea—until I find you.'

'That would be very brave of you, Lucy Goosey,'
said her mother.

'Are you ready to go now?'

'Ready!' said Lucy Goosey.

And away they flew,
into a never-ending sky full of stars.